Quiet Bunny

This book belongs to:

Giovannanna
McCorack

Quiet Bunny

To Nancy and Julie

Thanks to Nancy Kriebel, for inspiring me with your insight as a speech language pathologist to create an interactive story that targets sounds that are instrumental for early speech development and pre-reading/reading skills.

ISBN 978-0-545-24506-7

12 11 10 9 8 7 6 5 4 3 2 1   10 11 12 13 14 15/0

Printed in the U.S.A.   08

This edition first printing, January 2010

Quiet Bunny

Lisa McCue

SCHOLASTIC INC.
New York Toronto London Auckland
Sydney Mexico City New Delhi Hong Kong

tWeet–tWeet–tWeet–tWeet

Quiet Bunny loves the sounds of the forest.

He loves the morning sounds of happy birds singing. . . .

SHhhhhhhhhhhhhhhhhhhhhhh

He loves the afternoon sound of the breeze rustling the leaves.

SHHhhhhhhhhhhhhhhhhhhh

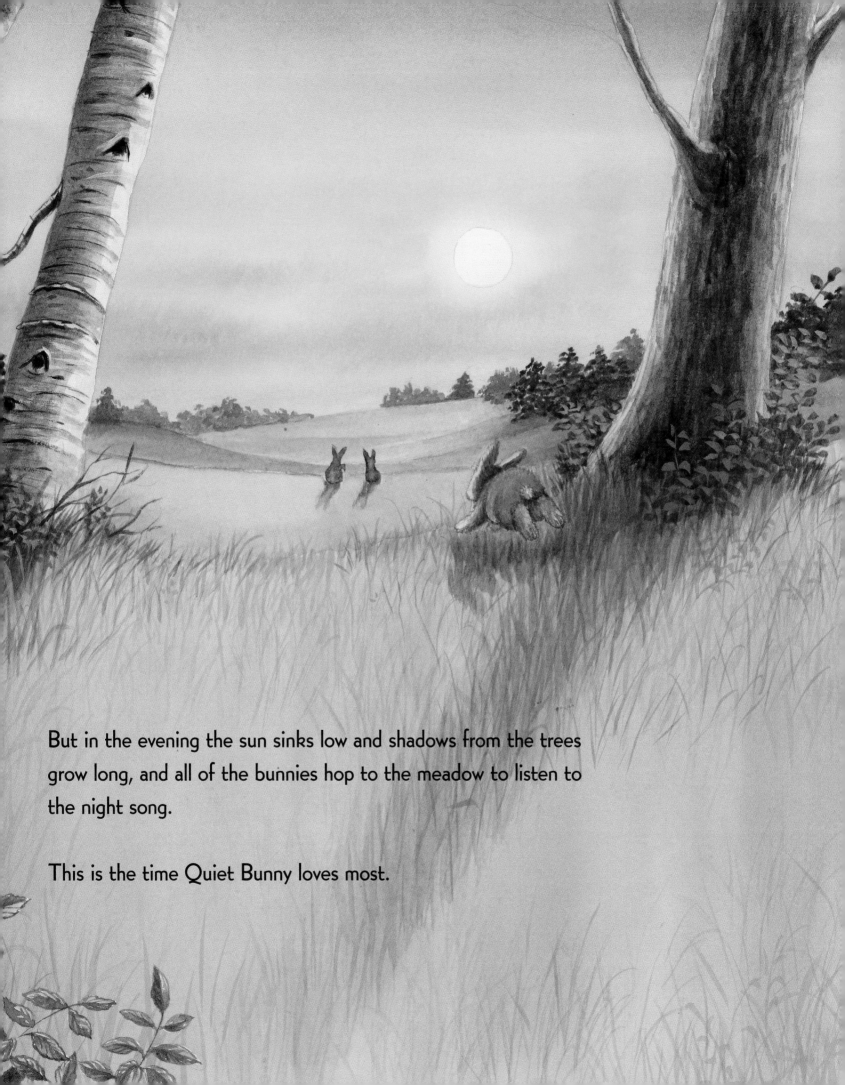

But in the evening the sun sinks low and shadows from the trees grow long, and all of the bunnies hop to the meadow to listen to the night song.

This is the time Quiet Bunny loves most.

Tonight Quiet Bunny did not sit up tall and still like the other bunnies. Instead, he lay back in the soft grass, closed his eyes, and spread his ears wide to listen as the animals started to sing.

nnNNNnnnnNNnnn

ch–CHEET
ch–CHEET
ch–CHEET

First the cricket, *ch-cheet ch-cheet ch-cheet.*

Then the owl, *hooooooooooooot, hooooooooooot.*

The snake, ssssssssssssssss.

And the tiny mosquitoes, *nNNnnnnnnnNnnn.*

He could hear the bullfrogs by the pond, *croak, croak, croak.*

And the wolf howling at the moon, *ouuuuuuuuu.*

Quiet Bunny longed to join in, but whenever he opened his mouth, no sound came out.

When the first star twinkled in the night sky, Quiet Bunny thought, *Tonight I will make a wish. I wish for a sound so that I can sing in the night song.*

The next morning, Quiet Bunny woke up early to the birds singing,

tWeet–tWeet–tweet

Excited, he opened his mouth to join in, but he was as quiet as ever.
If only my wish had come true, he thought, as he set off hopping
through the forest.

At the edge of the pond Quiet Bunny watched an enormous bull frog puff up his throat. Quiet Bunny tried to do the same. The bull frog bellowed,

CROaK
CrOAK

CROAK CROaK

Quiet Bunny was silent.

Across the pond wading in the rushes, was a tall loon with his head thrown back as he sang,

Quiet Bunny threw his head back too, opened his mouth and sang . . . nothing.

Down the path Quiet Bunny saw a snake curled up on a rock basking in the sun. The snake lifted her head and with a forked tongue she hissed,

Quiet Bunny could lift his head as high as the snake, but his little pink bunny tongue made no sound.

All day long Quiet Bunny hopped around the forest trying to hum like the hummingbirds,

HmmMmmmMm

growl like the bear cub,

Grrrrrrrrrrrrr

and buzz like the bees.

BzZzzzzZzzzZz

Zzzzz

As the day faded to dusk, a sad Quiet Bunny turned to head for the meadow.

Zoom! Overhead flew a bat,

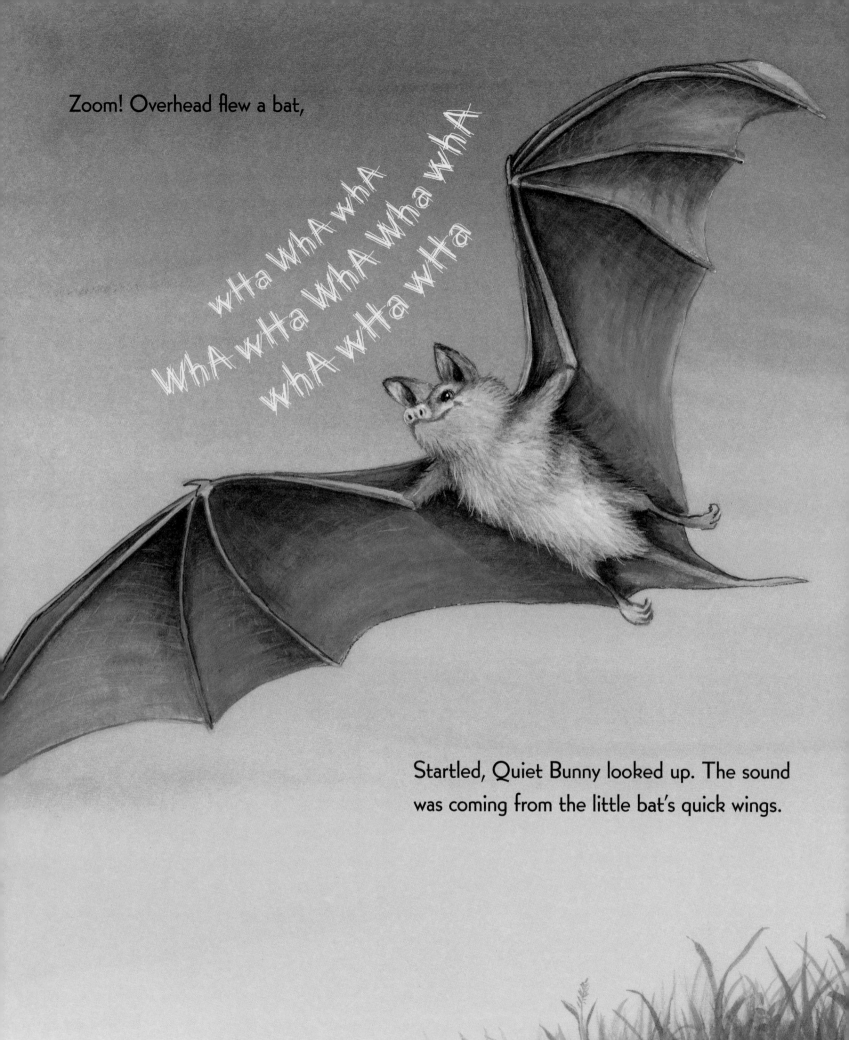

Startled, Quiet Bunny looked up. The sound was coming from the little bat's quick wings.

Quiet Bunny flapped his paws. No sound.

He flapped his ears. No sound.

He flapped his paws and his ears, but there was no
wha wha wha from this soft fuzzy bunny.

Quiet Bunny noticed a cricket sitting on a long blade of grass,
happily rubbing his hind legs together,

ch-CHeET ch-CHEET ch-CHEET

ch-C

Quiet Bunny was sure he could do this. He held up his big furry feet and started to rub them together. He rubbed and rubbed and rubbed and rubbed.

HEET ch-CHEET ch-CHEET

HOooooooT

Hooooooooot

Quiet Bunny stopped rubbing. Above him sat a large owl.

"I've been watching you, Quiet Bunny," said the owl. "It doesn't
matter how hard you rub your feet together, or flap your ears, or
puff up your cheeks, you will never make the sound of a cricket,
or a bat, or a frog. You are a Quiet Bunny. Be whoooooo you are,
and you will find your own bunny sound."

Who am I? Quiet Bunny wondered.

The wind whispered,   SHHhhhhhhhhhhhhhhhhh

Quiet Bunny wiggled his ears. "I am a bunny with large
floppy ears who loves to listen to the forest sounds."
Quiet Bunny blinked. "I am a bunny with curious eyes
who loves to watch the sunset."

SHhhhhhhhhhhhhhhhhhhhhhhh

Quiet Bunny twitched his nose. "I am a bunny who loves to sniff the sweet scent of honeysuckle."

Quiet Bunny wiggled his toes. "I am a bunny with big furry feet who loves to hop, and right now I must hop to the meadow or I will miss the start of the night song."

But right in Quiet Bunny's way was a big hollow log.
With a running start, Quiet Bunny leaped onto the log landing with a . . .

Had Quiet Bunny made a sound? He tapped his foot on the log again, tap, tap, tap, and again a loud *THUMP, THUMP, THUMP* came out. He had made a sound!

Quiet Bunny leaped with joy, and started to dance. *Thump, thump, thump,* he started to tap a beat. *Thump-da-dum, thump-thump-da–dum, thump-thump-da-dum, thump-thump.*

Soon Quiet Bunny was surrounded by the other animals coming to see who had started the night song with such a wonderful beat. One by one they started to join in. And a sweet melody filled the meadow.

LuluLuuLuLu LuluLuuLuLu

wHtawHta

HmmMmmm

BzZzzzz

Grrrrrrrrrrrrrrr

HUmP-da-DUM, tHuMp-tHUMp-da-dum

ch-CHEET
ch-CHEET

Next time you go outside on a warm summer night, listen closely.

You just might hear Quiet Bunny leading the night song.